rents

Your child is beginning the lifelong adventure of reading! And with the **World of Reading** program, you can be sure that he or she is receiving the encouragement needed to become a confident, independent reader. This program is specially designed to encourage your child to enjoy reading at every level by combining exciting, easy-to-read stories featuring favorite characters with colorful art that brings the magic to life.

The **World of Reading** program is divided into four levels so that children at any stage can enjoy a successful reading experience:

Reader-in-Training
Pre-K–Kindergarten
Picture reading and word repetition for children who are getting ready to read.

Beginner Reader
Pre-K–Grade 1
Simple stories and easy-to-sound-out words for children who are just learning to read.

Junior Reader
Kindergarten–Grade 2
Slightly longer stories and more varied sentences perfect for children who are reading with the help of a parent.

Super Reader
Grade 1–Grade 3
Encourages independent reading with rich storylines and wide vocabulary that's right for children who are reading on their own.

Learning to read is a once-in-a-lifetime adventure, and with **World of Reading**, the journey is just beginning!

Printed in the United States of America
First Edition
1 3 5 7 9 10 8 6 4 2
J689-1817-1-13182

ISBN 978-1-4231-6975-8

For more Disney Press fun, visit www.disneybooks.com
For more Buddies fun, visit www.disney.com/buddies

World of Reading

LEVEL 2

Disney Buddies

Budderball's First Fair

Written by Jodie Shepherd

Based on the character "Air Bud," created by Kevin DiCicco

Based on characters created by Robert Vince & Anna McRoberts

New York

It was opening day of the Fernfield Fair. The Buddies were very excited. It was their first fair.

“Mmm. I can smell the popcorn already!” Budderball said.
He licked his lips.
“Let’s go!”

Their first stop was
the petting zoo.
There were goats,
bunnies, sheep,
and even a llama!

Now there were puppies, too.
But Budderball was not happy.
"The food here is awful!" he said.
He spat out some hay.

There was so much more to see.
The Buddies decided to play
some games.
B-Dawg won the basketball toss.
He gave his prize to Rosebud.

Budderball passed by
a pickle toss game.
"I can't believe it!" he cried.
"These pickles are plastic."

Mudbud walked by a big glass tank.
Just then, a man scooped him up.
“You need a dip in the dunk tank,”
the man told Mudbud.

A boy threw a ball.
SPLASH!
Yuck! Mudbud was clean.
He climbed out
to find some dirt.

Buddha and Budderball
found a peaceful place.
Someone was playing a harmonica.
Buddha loved the melody.

Grumble rumble.
What was that new sound?
Budderball looked at Buddha.
"It's my tummy," Budderball said.

B-Dawg ran to a bouncy house.
"Way cool," he said.
"I've always wanted to try this."
He bounced up and down.

BOUNCE
BOUNCE BLAST

Rosebud was going
up and down, too.
From high up on the Ferris wheel,
she could see the whole fair.
She could see B-Dawg bouncing.

She could see Mudbud in the
animal tent.
He was with the cows and pigs.
The pigsty was the perfect place
for him!

She could see Buddha
at the bumper cars.
He was actually meditating.
His eyes were calmly closed.

All of Rosebud's brothers
were having so much fun.
But where was Budderball?

Budderball had found
the perfect spot for himself—
the food stalls.

He tried some french fries.
And some pizza.
And some cotton candy.

Then Budderball saw a sign:
PIE CONTEST.
"Awesome! Can I please be a judge?"

But the judging table was full.
"Sorry," said a woman.
"There's no room for you here."

But wait!
Budderball saw another sign:
PIE-EATING CONTEST.
That was even better!

This time, there was
an empty spot.
Budderball wiggled into place.
Ready, set, eat!

Budderball ate an apple pie.
He ate three blueberry pies.
He ate two pecan pies.
And he finished with a
banana cream pie.

"The winner!" announced
the head judge.
Budderball got a blue ribbon.
The crowd couldn't believe that
a puppy had finished all those pies!

Budderball stood onstage proudly.
Then he licked the last bit
of whipped cream from the floor.

Just then, his brothers
and sister ran up.
They cheered for him.
“Hooray for Budderball!”

As the Buddies left, they all agreed
it was a great fair.
"It was fantastic and food-tastic!"
Budderball added happily.